Hello, Family Members,

Learning to read is one of the most important accomplishments of early childhood. **Hello Reader!** books are designed to help children become skilled readers who like to read. Beginning readers learn to read by remembering frequently used words like "the," "is," and "and"; by using phonics skills to decode new words; and by interpreting picture and text clues. These books provide both the stories children enjoy and the structure they need to read fluently and independently. Here are suggestions for helping your child *before*, *during*, and *after* reading:

Before

- Look at the cover and pictures and have your child predict what the story is about.
- Read the story to your child.
- Encourage your child to chime in with familiar words and phrases.
- Echo read with your child by reading a line first and having your child read it after you do.

During

- Have your child think about a word he or she does not recognize right away. Provide hints such as "Let's see if we know the sounds" and "Have we read other words like this one?"
- Encourage your child to use phonics skills to sound out new words.
- Provide the word for your child when more assistance is needed so that he or she does not struggle and the experience of reading with you is a positive one.
- Encourage your child to have fun by reading with a lot of expression . . . like an actor!

After

- Have your child keep lists of interesting and favorite words.
- Encourage your child to read the books over and over again. Have him or her read to brothers, sisters, grandparents, and even teddy bears. Repeated readings develop confidence in young readers.
- Talk about the stories. Ask and answer questions. Share ideas about the funniest and most interesting characters and events in the stories.

I do hope that you and your child enjoy this book.

—Francie Alexander
Reading Specialist,
Scholastic's Learning Ventures

All Illustrations by Bob Doucet

Photographs appearing on the cover and pages 8, 16, 24, 30, 36,
and 42: © Royal Geographical Society, London, England; pages 4
and 46: © Scott Polar Research Institute, Cambridge, England.
Picture Research by Ferris Cook

ISBN: 0-439-20640-5
Text copyright © 2001 by Connie and Peter Roop.
Illustrations copyright © 2001 by Bob Doucet.
All rights reserved. Published by Scholastic Inc.
SCHOLASTIC, HELLO READER, CARTWHEEL BOOKS, and associated logos
are trademarks and/or registered trademarks of Scholastic Inc.

Library of Congress Cataloging-in-Publication Data
Roop, Connie.
    Escape from the ice: Shackleton and the endurance / by Connie and Peter Roop; illus-
trated by Bob Doucet.
        p.   cm.— (Hello reader! Level 4)
    Summary: Describes the events of the 1914 Shackleton Antarctic expedition when after
being trapped in a frozen sea for nine months, their ship, Endurance, was finally crushed,
forcing Shackleton and his men to make a very long and perilous journey across ice and
stormy seas to reach inhabited land.
    ISBN 0-439-20640-5 (pbk.)
    1. Shackleton, Ernest Henry, Sir, 1874-1922—Journeys—Juvenile literature. 2.
Endurance (Ship)—Juvenile literature.
    3. Antarctica—Discovery and exploration—Juvenile literature
[I. Shackleton, Ernest Henry, Sir, 1874-1922. 2. Explorers. 3. Antarctica—Discovery and explo-
ration. 4. Endurance (Ship) 5. Imperial Trans-Antarctic Expedition (1914-1917)] I. Roop, Peter.
II. Doucet, Bob. III. Title. IV. Series

G850 1914 .S53 R66 2000
919.8'904— dc21   00-026557

10 9 8 7 6 5 4 3 2 1   01 02 03 04 05

                        Printed in the U.S.A.
                    First printing, November 2001

ESCAPE FROM THE ICE

Shackleton and the *Endurance*

by Connie and Peter Roop
Illustrated by Bob Doucet

Hello Reader!—Level 4

SCHOLASTIC INC.
New York Toronto London Auckland Sydney
Mexico City New Delhi Hong Kong

CHAPTER ONE
Men Wanted for Hazardous Journey

Sir Ernest Shackleton needed twenty-seven brave men. He placed an advertisement in English newspapers.

"Men wanted for Hazardous Journey. Small wages, bitter cold, long months of complete darkness, constant danger, safe return doubtful. Honour and recognition in case of success."

5,000 men applied!

What was Shackleton's "Hazardous Journey"? The Imperial Trans-Antarctic Expedition, his third visit to the frozen continent of Antarctica.

In 1902, Shackleton had sailed to Antarctica aboard the *Discovery* with explorer Robert Scott. Shackleton, Scott, and Edmund Wilson, another explorer, marched for three months across snow and ice. They wanted to be the first to reach the South Pole. They failed, and Shackleton almost died.

In 1907, Shackleton led his own expedition to Antarctica. He came within ninety-seven miles of the South Pole, a new record. For his accomplishments, Ernest Shackleton was knighted. Sir Ernest was famous for his courage and determination.

In 1911, Robert Scott searched again for the South Pole. Shackleton was not with him. When Scott reached the pole, he found the Norwegian flag flying. Roald Amundsen, a Norwegian explorer, had beaten Scott. Returning, Scott and his men died from cold and hunger.

Now that the South Pole had been reached, Shackleton formed another goal: to cross Antarctica. His expedition would ski, hike, sled, and climb to the South Pole. They would continue to McMurdo Sound.

No one had ever attempted such a journey. Antarctica's temperature dropped to 129 degrees Fahrenheit below zero. One hundred mile per hour winds howled. Blinding snowstorms raged. Crossing Antarctica's 1,500 miles of glaciers, mountains, ice fields, and unknown dangers seemed impossible.

Not to Sir Ernest Shackleton. He believed in the determined "nature of British courage." He intended to cross Antarctica or die trying.

With the right men, the strongest sled dogs, supplies to last two years, and a sturdy ship, Shackleton believed he would succeed.

Thus it was that 28 men, nearly 100 dogs, and two pigs boarded the ship *Endurance* in 1914. Joining the crew was Mrs. Chippy, the carpenter's cat.

No one knew *Endurance* was on a journey of no return.

CHAPTER TWO
Trapped by the Ice!

Endurance had been built especially for travel through ice. Her bow was four feet thick to push away ice. She had three masts for sailing and a coal-burning engine.

Below deck, *Endurance* was crowded with sleds, ropes, guns, barrels of food, casks of fresh water, skis, rifles, ammunition, spare clothes, and hundreds of other things needed to survive once the group reached Antarctica.

The deck was crowded, too. Dog kennels were built. Coal was piled high.

As the men prepared the ship, Frank Hurley, the expedition photographer, recorded their efforts on film. His photos and film captured the struggles and hardships Shackleton, the ship, and her crewmen would endure.

On December 5, 1914, *Endurance* steamed away from South Georgia Island, the last outpost before Antarctica. The sky was overcast. The men were excited. The long days of preparation were over. The real adventure was beginning. *Endurance* turned south and dipped into the ocean swells. Civilization and safety fell behind.

The Weddell Sea, stretching hundreds of miles from Antarctica's ice-bound shores, was the crew's first destination.

"What welcome was the Weddell Sea preparing for us?" wondered and worried Sir Ernest.

The whalers on South Georgia Island had warned Shackleton of early ice. They told him he must force his way through heavy pack ice to reach land.

Pack ice is a gigantic jigsaw puzzle. Some chunks are huge, others small. Many are sharp-edged. The wind and water breaks the ice apart, then smashes it back together. Icebergs drift in the pack ice. Two years earlier, an iceberg had sunk the "unsinkable" *Titanic*.

On December 7, two days into the voyage, *Endurance* encountered ice. Shackleton was surprised to find ice so far north in the Antarctic summer.

Endurance, dodging icebergs seventy feet high and five miles long, split the ice with her strong bow, slowly shouldering her way through.

When not watching for ice, the men enjoyed gazing at the ocean animals. Penguins leaped. Seals snorted. Terns, gulls, and albatrosses whirled overhead. Whales spouted.

By Christmas, the crew had steamed hundreds of miles into the pack ice. On Christmas Day alone they covered seventy-one miles. To celebrate, the men enjoyed a delicious meal of soup, rabbit, fish, pudding, and fruit. Leonard Hussey, the ship's weatherman and musician, led a "sing-song" on his homemade one-string violin.

By New Year's Day, they had muscled their way 480 miles through the pack ice.

Just after New Year's, *Endurance* covered 124 miles in one day. Shackleton hoped to see land soon. He was eager to be on shore so the men and dogs could exercise.

One day, the men ran the dogs on the ice. They watched for water, holes, cracks, and killer whales. The hungry whales hunted seals by tipping over the ice and plunging the unlucky seal into the sea. To the whales, a man or a dog was the same as a seal meal.

Once, while playing ice soccer, Captain Frank Worsley fell into a hole. Fortunately, he was rescued along with the ball!

Trouble began. They tried to steer south, but the only open water was north, behind them. Shackleton refused to reverse his course. He said, "It was as though the spirits of the Antarctic were pointing us to the backward track, the track we determined not to follow."

By January 10, the ice was thicker. The weather grew worse. Gales followed blizzards. Glaciers sliding off Antarctica blocked their way.

On January 17, Shackleton ordered *Endurance* anchored to a small iceberg. A storm raged. When it cleared, the ship was surrounded by ice.

Endurance could not move forward. She could not move backward.

Endurance was trapped in the ice!

CHAPTER THREE
"What the Ice Gets, the Ice Keeps"

"What the ice gets, the ice keeps," Sir Shackleton told Captain Worsley.

For a month, the men struggled to break the *Endurance* out of the ice. They chopped channels in the ice. *Endurance* tried to smash through. It was no use. The icy grip held her firm.

On February 24, 1915, Shackleton changed his plans. *Endurance* would be a winter station. The men would work days. They would sleep nights. Meals would be at regular times.

The dogs were taken off the *Endurance*. "Dogloos" (like igloos) were built for them on the ice. The men trained the dogs to pull sleds. They raced them on flat ice. There was good-natured rivalry between teams of men and dogs.

The men played ice hockey and ice soccer. They hunted seals for meat for the dogs and themselves. They saved the blubber for fuel because their supply of coal was running low.

They collected information on weather, water, and sealife. They dropped nets through holes to collect fish. They played with a litter of newborn puppies. And they searched for a path to freedom.

Sir Ernest kept the men busy. They would not have time to worry about danger and death.

Even trapped in the ice, *Endurance* moved. When she was first trapped in January 1915, the expedition was within 100 miles of the shores of Antarctica. Now the ice holding the ship shifted and drifted north.

Shackleton was concerned. Winter was coming. Temperatures were dropping. Seals and birds were leaving. Storms were frequent. "Where would the vagrant winds and currents carry the ship during the long winter months?" Shackleton worried.

Each day the men worked, played, and searched. Each day the sun set earlier and earlier.

The men marveled at Antarctica's wonders: The ice cracked, creaked, groaned, grunted, squeaked, and squealed. Sometimes it sounded like screeching birds. Other times it whistled like steam kettles. Huge chunks would pop into the air, flip over, and crash back down.

The men enjoyed wonderful mirages. Land suddenly appeared where there was no land. Icebergs floated in the sky. Ice cliffs doubled and tripled. The sun seemed to set and return. The men knew these were visual tricks of the air, land, and water.

The winds blew stronger. The nights grew longer. The blizzards became more violent. *Endurance* drifted farther from the Antarctic shore.

"We said good-bye to the sun on May 1," Shackleton wrote. The sun would not shine on them for seventy days. "All hands are cheery and busy, and will do the best when the time for action comes. In the meantime we must wait."

Frank Hurley took many pictures. He rigged lights to photograph during the long Antarctic night. The lights would also help if the ice cracked and the remaining dogs had to be rushed on board.

On May 15, the crew held a special competition, the Antarctic Derby Dogsled Race. The racetrack was 700 yards long. Five teams started. The men on the sidelines cheered even though they couldn't see the teams until the finish line. Captain Worsley was the winner!

On May 22, the men celebrated Midwinter's Day. The new moon shone. Little work was done. The cook prepared his best dishes. The men made speeches and sang. They wished each other success no matter what happened.

By early July, the men saw beautiful sunrises. Twilight lasted longer than before. The ice cracked more often. The long winter night was ending.

Then the worst blizzard struck. Winds roared at seventy miles per hour. *Endurance* trembled under its attack. But the men were snug on the ship. The dogs huddled in the dogloos.

Hundreds of tons of snow piled up against *Endurance*. Millions of tons of ice squeezed the ship until her timbers groaned. Was this more than the sturdy ship could endure?

On August 1, exactly a year after *Endurance* left London, the ice split open!

The dogs were brought on board. The crew's spirits soared. Were they free at last?

The crack closed again. Ice smacked against the ship. It pushed against the sides. The wood creaked and cracked. Ice popped into the air.

Shackleton worried about the ship's rudder. If ice broke it, they would not be able to steer the ship.

On September 2, the ship jumped. She groaned and moaned as the ice shoved against her. For over a month, the men watched and waited and wondered.

Would the ice keep what it caught?

The deck shuddered. The wood bent. Every man was ready for disaster.

Endurance endured. She had fought the ice for ten months. But how much longer could she fight?

Summer in Antarctica was coming. Would it arrive soon enough?

Shackleton ordered the men to abandon the ship. They took food, coal, and clothes. They built a camp on the ice.

From a safe distance they watched *Endurance* slowly be crushed.

CHAPTER FOUR
Life on the Ice

"The task was to secure the safety of the party," Shackleton wrote. To survive, "I must apply every bit of knowledge experience of the Antarctic has given me."

Shackleton knew he would need knowledge and luck. The nearest shelter was a hut with emergency supplies on Paulet Island. But it was 350 miles away.

The men hurried, not knowing when *Endurance* might slip through the ice. They saved anything from the ship which might help them survive an Antarctic winter. Dumping the supplies a short distance from the ship, they nicknamed their first camp on the ice "Dump Camp."

The men and dogs had enough food to last for fifty-six days. If they shot seals, their food supply would last longer. Shackleton ordered any "weaklings" among the animals to be shot because they would starve to death. The men could not afford to feed pets. Mrs. Chippy, the ship's cat, and three dogs were

first. The men were sad but understood Shackleton's order. They had to do everything they could to survive.

Shackleton worried. Should they remain on the drifting ice? Or should they pull the three boats over the ice to reach land?

Shackleton decided to march to land. The men made sleds for their three lifeboats: the *James Caird*, the *Dudley Docker,* and the *Stancomb-Wills.* The dogs and men would pull the boats.

Each man was allowed to carry only two pounds of personal things. The men dug "little white graves" in the snow to bury other personal items. Hurley, the photographer, had to leave many of his pictures behind. The glass plates on which they were preserved weighed too much.

The men and dogs dragged the three boats six miles the first day. They moved one mile forward. The other five miles were spent dodging ridges and holes.

They traveled a half mile the second day. The temperature rose. The ice groaned. The third day the men sank to their hips in the snow. They went one-quarter mile before stopping.

Dragging the boats exhausted the men. The thinning ice was dangerous. Ocean Camp was set up on a raft of thick ice. This floating ice raft was their home for the next two months.

Men returned to Dump Camp to collect clothes and food. They dug up the "little white graves." They took anything they could from *Endurance*, including three tons of food. Hurley even dove into the icy water to rescue his photos from inside the ship.

To pass the time, the men read, exercised, talked, sang, hunted, walked, and slept. They practiced packing up the camp until they could do it in five minutes. This was in case the ice suddenly broke beneath them.

Breakfast was fried seal. Dinner was "hoosh," penguin stew. After dinner most men slept. Each night some stayed awake. They watched to make sure the ice did not crack and set men or dogs drifting away.

They also kept an eye on *Endurance*. Ever so slowly, she was sinking. Finally, on November 15, 1915, *Endurance* gave up her battle with the ice. Bow down, stern up, she sank forever beneath the ice.

Shackleton said, "She's gone, boys," as the ship disappeared. The men's spirits dropped. Silence settled over Ocean Camp. Shackleton ordered extra food for dinner. "Soon everyone was cheery as usual," wrote Shackleton.

Summer was returning. The temperatures warmed. Ice cracked into channels. Shackleton decided to push on again.

The men celebrated Christmas early, on December 22. They feasted on fish, baked beans, rabbit, and any remaining treats. They ate all they could, because much of the uneaten food would be left behind. Unknown to the men, this was to be their last good meal for eight months.

The crew set off. The going was tough and the snow was soft. The men often fell into holes. One day they traveled only 200 yards.

Shackleton ordered Patience Camp set up on another thick ice raft. Here they lived for three months.

CHAPTER FIVE
Escape from the Ice

Food ran low. The men had one hot drink each day. They were tired and weak.

The food rations in the boats were not touched. These had to be saved for when the men found open water.

By March, the men were eating seal blubber. One man wrote, "It will do us all good to be hungry like this, for we will appreciate so much more the good things when we get home."

Even with *Endurance* gone, the men still hoped to reach home. Someday.

The dogs were as hungry and as weak as the men. Shackleton made another hard decision. The dogs must be shot before they starved to death. Early in April, the last of the dog teams were gone.

The ice began breaking up. But it was not enough to launch the boats. Whenever the ice finally opened, Shackleton and his men planned to sail 100 miles to Elephant Island.

Each day, the ice under Patience Camp shrank. Soon Patience Camp would break apart.

On April 9, a crack in the ice opened right where Sir Shackleton had slept for months! If it had split while he was sleeping, he would have fallen in the sea.

The twenty-eight men got into the boats. They rowed through the ice-filled water. As darkness came, they reached a flat ice raft. They set up camp, ate, and slept.

Shackleton stayed awake to write in his journal. Suddenly he felt uneasy.

He went for a walk to check the camp. All at once, the ice split beneath a tent. Shackleton reached down and grabbed a sinking sleeping bag. He pulled it out just as the ice crashed together again. The man in the bag was wet, but alive.

No one slept the rest of the night. Killer whales circled the ice raft. The men waited for dawn. Finally, it came. They launched the boats again.

They reached open water. The heavy boats rode low in the water. Salt spray splashed the men and froze. The boats would sink if covered with too much ice. The tired men tied up to an iceberg to chip off the ice.

Shackleton watched and waited. He saw a large gap through the ice. The men rushed back into the boats. They rowed all day and into the night. Rain and snow fell. Killer whales circled.

The men tried to be cheerful. But they were cold, hungry, tired, and losing hope. Would they ever set foot on land again?

When night fell, they tied the boats together. Ice hit them as they drifted all night. Some men had frostbitten fingers. Some were seasick. Their beards were white with frost. On they sailed.

Finally, the ice ended. Ahead rolled open ocean. At last they were free of the hated ice!

But they had a new enemy now—thirst. For months they had melted ice to drink. Now they had no ice to melt. Their tongues became swollen. Never before had they been so uncomfortable.

Would they live to reach land?

At last they neared Elephant Island. Shooting through the breaking waves, the boats beached on the rocky shore. The men laughed and cried. They held up handfuls of pebbles and let them trickle through their fingers. They had not set foot on land since leaving South Georgia Island sixteen months before.

They had escaped the ice! They had faced danger and death. But Shackleton worried. Were they now to die on Elephant Island?

No! He would go for help. He would take one boat and five men. They would sail to South Georgia Island. He would get help at the whaling station and return for the other twenty-two men.

Sir Ernest Shackleton would never give up.

He only had to cross 800 miles of the worst seas in the world.

CHAPTER SIX
The Voyage of the *Caird*

The *James Caird* was prepared for the voyage. The carpenter covered her open deck with wood and canvas. Food was stored with 250 pounds of ice for water.

The work was difficult. Blizzards raged. The wind was so strong it knocked the men down.

Finally, everything was ready. The *Caird* was launched. Six men sailed aboard her.

The men staying behind waved from the shore. They gave three cheers. As the *Caird* sailed away, their hopes for rescue sailed with her.

For sixteen days and nights, the *Caird* battled the wind, weather, and waves. Spray soaked the men's clothes. The boat leaked. Nothing was dry or warm. Snow and rain fell. Winds roared around them. Huge waves surged under them.

Shackleton and his crew bravely sailed on. Knowing they were traveling over sixty miles a day lifted their spirits. Meals were bright spots in the dreary days and nights.

One day, ice formed on the *Caird*, threatening to sink her. The ice was chipped away. "The *James Caird* lifted to the endless waves as if she lived again," Sir Ernest later wrote.

That afternoon the sun shone. Sleeping bags and clothes were hung to dry. A hot meal was enjoyed. They were halfway through their voyage to get help.

"We were a tiny speck in the vast waste of the

sea," Shackleton wrote. But they were alive. And they had hope.

One midnight, Shackleton was steering. He looked up at the biggest wave he had ever seen!

"Hold on!" he shouted. "It's got us!" The boat was tossed like a cork. Water crashed down on them, half flooding the *Caird*.

The men bailed with all their remaining energy. The *Caird* floated safely again. Another danger had been conquered.

On they sailed. Water ran low. Thirst became their enemy again. The tortured days and nights slowly passed.

One morning the men spotted seaweed. Two shags, birds which rarely flew fifteen miles from land, passed by.

Ahead were the jagged cliffs of South Georgia Island!

Forty-foot waves crashed against the shore. Towering cliffs dropped straight into the sea. Had they come this far, and suffered so much, only to be wrecked on the rocks?

The crew sailed away from shore as far as they could. They spent the night tossing on the waves. The next day the wind blew them toward shore. They could not escape. The wind pushed them on and on.

Suddenly, the wind dropped. They drifted away from the deadly rocks.

Another day and night passed before they saw a crack in the cliffs. With Shackleton carefully steering, the *Caird* shot between two rocky reefs. They glided onto a beach.

The men struggled ashore. South Georgia Island at last! Wonder of wonders: A stream of fresh water flowed at their feet.

Sir Shackleton looked up at the mountains looming over them. He had only to cross them to reach the whaling station. No one had crossed them before. He had no idea of the dangers and difficulties ahead. But as always, Sir Shackleton was determined to succeed.

CHAPTER SEVEN
Rescue!

Three of the men were too sick and tired to cross the island. After resting, Sir Shackleton, Captain Worsley, and First Officer Thomas Crean set off for the whaling station. Each carried fifty feet of rope and a sock filled with food. Screws from the *Caird* were stuck into their boots to help them grip the slippery ice.

Shackleton guessed they had only seventeen miles to hike. He did not know it was thirty miles over icy mountains. But he knew help for the twenty-two men stranded on Elephant Island lay on the other side.

The three men climbed up and down mountains. They hiked over and around glaciers. Their legs ached, for they had done no walking for a long time.

They reached the top of a mountain late that afternoon. Storm clouds raced their way. They did not have a tent or sleeping bags. If the storm caught them on the mountain, they would die.

Using their ropes, they made a sled. Not knowing if cliffs lay ahead, they rocketed down the mountain and crashed into a snowbank. Laughing, they walked on.

Sometimes, they went the wrong way and had to retrace their steps. They were exhausted. Shackleton let the others sleep only five minutes at a time. To fall sound asleep could bring on death.

Finally, they saw the whaling station. One man said, "Boss, it looks too good to be true." Then they heard a steam whistle. "Never before had any of us heard sweeter music," Shackleton wrote. The whistle meant men. Men meant rescue!

They saw a ship and tiny men far below. Shackleton, Worsley, and Crean shook hands at their success.

One last challenge blocked their way—a towering waterfall! Using their ropes, they slid down through the freezing water. Shivering, yet happy, they hurried to the whaling station.

They first met two young boys. The boys were frightened at these smelly, dirty men, and ran away. Next, Shackleton and his companions met a man. He ran away, too. Was this their welcome, after all the suffering?

At a house, Shackleton asked for his friend Mr. Sorlle. At first, Sorlle did not recognize Shackleton. When he did, the welcome was wonderful!

Shackleton and his men were warmed and fed. They were cleaned and given new clothes. They were told of the millions of young men dying in the war in Europe.

Sorlle sent a whaling ship to rescue the three men on the other side of the island. Captain Worsley went with the ship. When he reached them, the men did not recognize him, clean and in new clothes!

Carefully, they loaded the faithful *James Caird* onto the whaling ship. Today, the *James Caird* is on display in England. People gaze at her in admiration for making the 800-mile journey across such terrible seas.

The whalers eagerly helped Sir Shackleton prepare a ship, the *Southern Sky*, to rescue the men on Elephant Island. The ship was no *Endurance*. She could fight waves, but not ice. Within seventy miles of Elephant Island, they were forced to go back.

Shackleton would not give up. He got another ship. Ice again stopped him.

Yet another ship also failed. On the fourth attempt, after four long months, Sir Ernest Shackleton reached his twenty-two stranded men. All were alive. They had survived by eating seals and living under their boats.

They were rescued at last!

CHAPTER EIGHT
The End of the Story

Sir Ernest Shackleton and his men had set out to accomplish something no one else ever had: crossing Antarctica.

Instead, they accomplished something even greater. With determination, humor, strength, and willpower, they survived two years of danger, hunger, and cold. They proved to themselves and to the world what men could do under Antarctica's harsh conditions.

Shackleton and his men returned to a world gone mad. While they were fighting to survive, millions of men were fighting a terrible war. On their return, some of Shackleton's men joined the army and navy. Some died in battle. Others lived through the war. Others sailed the seas again.

Sir Shackleton's dreams of Antarctica did not die. In 1921, he set out to return to Antarctica. This time he would sail around the continent. He would map all of the islands.

But the strain of his three Antarctic adventures had injured his health. On January 5, 1922, Sir Ernest Shackleton had a heart attack and died. Beneath a monument of stones, he was buried on South Georgia Island.

Shackleton's dream lives on. Each year men and women brave Antarctica's dangers. They are scientists and explorers determined to learn more about the frozen world at the end of the earth.

Just as Sir Ernest Shackleton dreamed of doing. And did.

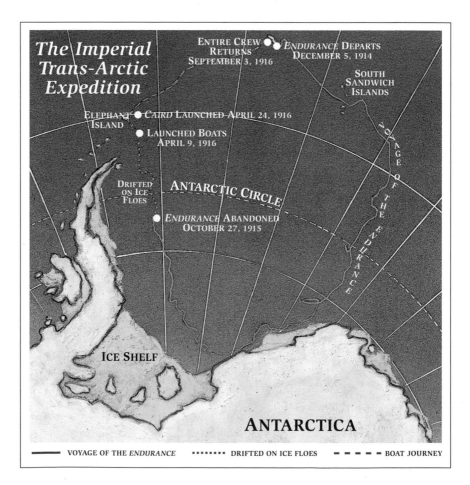

The Imperial Trans-Arctic Expedition

ENTIRE CREW RETURNS SEPTEMBER 3, 1916

ENDURANCE DEPARTS DECEMBER 5, 1914

SOUTH SANDWICH ISLANDS

ELEPHANT ISLAND

CAIRD LAUNCHED APRIL 24, 1916

LAUNCHED BOATS APRIL 9, 1916

VOYAGE OF THE ENDURANCE

DRIFTED ON ICE FLOES

ANTARCTIC CIRCLE

ENDURANCE ABANDONED OCTOBER 27, 1915

ICE SHELF

ANTARCTICA

━━━━━ VOYAGE OF THE *ENDURANCE*   ·········· DRIFTED ON ICE FLOES   ▬ ▬ ▬ ▬ BOAT JOURNEY